THE MASTER & THE PROMISE

"I don't know why he's doing this, or how he can even *be*," Zee said. "I don't understand it at all. Hobgoblins are like a myth to us, something to terrify naughty children. The legend says that they were created by the first great goblin king of France—they were then lutins' servants and the king's bodyguards before they trained trolls. But the king had to kill them all because they were too violent and they tried to overthrow him. I thought they were all dead. That's what they taught us—that King Gofimbel and the Dark Faerie Queen executed them all."

She swallowed, then continued. "But this one isn't dead. And he hates goblins. Humans, too. The rage in him was so terrible that I fainted in the parking lot. The children had to drag me away from the mall—away from his aura. It was like I had breathed in his poison, his hate—and he saw me. Nick, he looked inside and knew who and what I am. He knew about the children, too, and wanted them."

Nick reached for Zee's hands, folded them in his own and brought them up to his mouth, where he breathed over their chilled flesh. He rubbed her skin lightly, part of him marveling at its texture.

"Don't worry." He looked into her eyes. They were different—beautiful, but not human—he could see that now. And it didn't matter. "We'll find your Jack Frost and we'll stop this monster. Then I will take you and the children far away to someplace safe where no one bad will ever find you."